Alice in Wonderland made Simple for Kids
Adopted from the original by Lewis Carroll
with all of the Original Drawings by John Tenniel

Alice was sitting next to her sister who was reading from a book. Alice did not like the book because it had no pictures in it. Alice was playing with her cat. Alice was sleepy.

Alice saw a White Rabbit with pink eyes run by. The White Rabbit was wearing a coat. The White Rabbit took a watch out of his pocket and looked at it. The White Rabbit said, "Oh Dear! Oh Dear! I shall be late."

The White Rabbit ran off. Alice was surprised because she had never seen a rabbit do this. Alice followed the White Rabbit into a rabbit hole.

Soon Alice was falling down, down, down.

Alice landed in a pile of leaves. She was not hurt.

Alice looked around. She was in a room with many doors, but all of the doors were locked.

There was a table in the room with a golden key on it, but the key did not fit into any of the locks.

Alice saw a curtain. Behind the curtain she found a small door. The golden key fit into the lock in the small door.

Alice opened the door with the key. The door was too small for Alice but she could see through the door. There was a beautiful garden on the other side of the door.

Alice went back to the table and saw a bottle that had not been there before. The bottle had the words "DRINK ME" on it

Alice put the key back on the table. Alice drank from the bottle. Alice became very small. Now she was small enough to go through the door to the beautiful garden.

But now the door was locked. Alice had left the key on the table. Now, Alice was too small to get the key off the table.

Then, Alice found a little box under the table. Alice opened the box. A small cake was inside. Alice ate the cake.

Suddenly, Alice grew very big. Now, she was ten feet tall.

Alice did not know what to do. She started to cry and cry.

Alice saw the White Rabbit. The White Rabbit walked past her, carrying white gloves. The White Rabbit said, "Oh! The Lady will be angry if I have made her wait."

Alice called to the White Rabbit but he did not answer.

Alice picked up the bottle on the table and drank from the bottle again.

Alice became very small. Alice found a white glove that had been dropped by the White Rabbit. Alice had left the key on the table. Alice had eaten all the cake. Now, she had no way out.

Alice had been crying all this time and now the floor was covered with her tears. Alice slipped and fell in the water.

Alice started swimming in the water. She saw a mouse swimming there too.

Alice tried to speak to the mouse. The mouse spoke back to her. Alice wanted to be friends with the mouse. She told the mouse what a nice cat Alice had. The mouse became scared and swam away.

Alice called to the mouse and told him that her cat was not here. Finally, the mouse came swimming back.

Soon, there were other animals in the water, a Duck, a Dodo and many strange animals.

Alice led the way, and the whole party swam to shore.

All the animals and Alice had a meeting. They decided that they had to get dry. They decided to have a race. They would run in a circle until they were dry.

The animals ran in a circle. When all the animals were dry, they stopped the race. They said that now there must be a prize. They said that Alice should give the prizes.

Alice had some candy in her pocket. She gave one piece of candy to each animal as a prize.

The Dodo asked Alice if she had anything else. Alice said that she had only one thimble. The Dodo took the thimble. Then, the Dodo gave the thimble back to Alice as a prize.

Alice said that she wished that her cat was here. All of the animals became afraid of the cat and ran or flew away.

The White Rabbit came back looking for the glove that he had lost.

The White Rabbit did not know who Alice was. He thought that Alice was his maid. He told Alice to go to his house and bring his gloves.

Alice did not want to tell the White Rabbit that he had made a mistake. She went inside the house to get the gloves.

Alice found the gloves. She also found a bottle. The bottle did not have anything written on it. Alice decided to drink the bottle anyway.

Alice became very big, so big that she could not get out of the house.

Alice heard the White Rabbit outside of the house looking for his gloves. He kept saying, "The Lady, the Lady, she will have me killed if I can not find the gloves".

The White Rabbit came to the door and called for his gloves. Alice was so big inside the house that the White Rabbit could not open the door.

The White Rabbit went around to the window. The White Rabbit tried to climb in the window. Alice reached out the window and tried to grab the White Rabbit. The White Rabbit screamed and ran away.

Just then, the maid arrived. The White Rabbit had thought that Alice was the maid. When the real maid arrived, they knew that somebody else was inside the house.

The White Rabbit called a lizard named Bill and told him to go down the chimney. Bill did not want to go down the chimney, but the White Rabbit made him go. Alice heard them talk about this.

When Bill came down the chimney, Alice gave a kick and sent Bill flying up into the air.

The White Rabbit and all the other animals decided to burn the house down. When Alice heard about this, she called out to them that she would call her cat. She thought that this would make them all afraid.

The animals threw a bucket of cakes in the window. Alice had an idea. She ate one of the cakes. It made her small again. Alice came out the door.

Alice ran away into the woods. Alice found a puppy dog there. It was a cute puppy, but Alice decided that she had better get away from it.

Alice found a big mushroom, as big as herself. She looked on top of the mushroom. She saw a blue caterpillar smoking a long pipe.

"Who are you?", said the Caterpillar.

"I do not know", said Alice. "I know who I was this morning, but I have changed so many times today I do not know who I am now."

"Who are you?", said the Caterpillar again.

Alice thought that she could not answer this question any better, so she started to walk away.

"Come back", said the Caterpillar. "I have something important to tell you."

Alice came back, because she thought the Caterpillar might have something important to say.

The Caterpillar read her a funny poem about an old man with white hair who liked to stand on his head because he was sure that he did not have a brain.

The old man was very fat but he liked to do a flip over his back.

The old man could eat an entire goose with beak and bones because his jaw muscles had become strong from arguing with his wife.

His eyes were so steady that he could balance an eel on the end of his nose.

When the story was finished, Alice thought she had heard enough. The Caterpillar asked her what she wanted. Alice said that she wanted to be bigger, as she was only three inches tall, the same size as the Caterpillar.

The Caterpillar put down his pipe, got off the mushroom, and crawled off into the grass, saying, "One side will make you larger. The other side will make you small."

"One side of what?", said Alice.

"Of the mushroom", said the Caterpillar, and he crawled away and disappeared.

Alice did not know what to do. Alice wanted to be bigger, but she did not know which side of the mushroom to eat.

Finally, Alice decided to take a chance and take a bite from one side of the mushroom.

Suddenly, Alice got smaller and smaller. If she did not do something quickly, she would be too small to eat anything.

Just in time, Alice grabbed a piece from the other side of the mushroom and ate it. Alice started growing bigger and bigger, so big that she was taller than the tallest trees.

Just then a pigeon flew by the top of the trees looking for a place to build her next. She wanted to build her nest at the top of a tall tree so that a snake would not eat her eggs. Alice now had a long neck, so the pigeon thought that she was a snake.

"I am not a snake. I am a little girl", said Alice.

Alice remembered that she had a piece of each side of the mushroom in her hands. She started eating a little bit of the one that makes you smaller and then a little bit of the one that makes you bigger.

Finally, she got herself down to her original size, which was four feet tall.

Now, Alice started looking for the beautiful garden, the same garden she first saw when she got to the bottom of the rabbit hole.

Alice saw a little house only four feet high. She decided to make herself nine inches tall, which was the right size for the house.

A fish dressed like a delivery man came to the house and knocked on the door.

A frog dressed like a butler opened the door and came out.

The fish carried a big letter, as big as himself, and handed it to the frog, saying, "An invitation to the Lady to play croquet with the Queen."

The frog took the letter and said, "From the Queen, an invitation to the Lady to play croquet."

The fish left. The door closed. Alice went to the door. Just as Alice got to the door, the door came open and out came a plate that had been thrown. Alice went inside the door.

The Lady was sitting there on a chair holding a baby that was crying and screaming. The room was filled with smoke. A cook was cooking. A cat was sitting on the floor with a big smile on its face.

"Why is the cat smiling?", asked Alice.

"Because it is a Cheshire Cat", said the Lady.

"I did not know cats could smile", said Alice.

"Most of them do", said the Lady. "Mind your business. Everybody minding their own business will make the world go round faster".

"Here, you may nurse it", said the Lady, handing the baby to Alice.

Alice took the baby. The Lady said, "I must go to play croquet with the Queen", and she left the house.

Alice looked at the baby and saw that it was not a baby but a pig. Alice took the pig outside, put it on the ground, and the pig walked off into the woods.

Alice looked up at a tree and saw the Cheshire Cat sitting up in the branches, grinning at her.

"Would you tell me which way to go?", said Alice.

"That depends on where you want to go", said the Cheshire Cat.

"I want to go anywhere", said Alice.

"Then it does not matter which way you go", said the Cheshire Cat.

"What kind of people are here?", asked Alice

"That way is the Mad Hatter. The other way is the March Hair. They are both mad", said the Cheshire Cat.

" I do not want to be with people who are mad", said Alice.

"You cannot help that. We are all mad here. I am mad. You are mad", said the Cheshire Cat.

" How do you know that I am mad?", said Alice.

"Because if you were not mad, you would not have come here", said the Cheshire Cat.

"Will you come today to play croquet with the queen?", asked the Cheshire Cat.

"I would like to", said Alice.

"You will see me there", said the Cheshire Cat. Then, the Cheshire Cat and faded away and disappeared.

Soon, the Cheshire Cat appeared again.

"What happened to the Baby?", the Cheshire Cat asked.

"It turned into a pig", said Alice.

"I thought it would", said the Cheshire Cat.

The Cheshire Cat disappeared again.

Soon, the Cheshire Cat appeared a third time. "I wish you would not appear and disappear so suddenly", said Alice.

"Okay. Next time I will disappear slowly", replied the Cheshire Cat. Then the Cheshire Cat faded slowly away, leaving only his teeth grinning at Alice.

"I have seen a cat without a grin, but I have never seen a grin without a cat", thought Alice.

Alice walked a little way and then she saw a house. It was a big house, so she ate a bit of the mushroom to make herself two feet tall.

There was a long table in front of the house. The Mad Hatter and the March Hair were sitting at one end of the table having a tea party. A dormouse was sitting between them, but he was fast asleep.

The long table had many chairs, but all three of them were sitting at one end of it. "No room. No room", the Mad Hatter cried as Alice came to the table.

"There is plenty of room", Alice said and sat down in one of the chairs.

"Would you like some wine?", asked the March Hair.

"I do not see any", said Alice.

"There is none", said the March Hair.

"Why did you offer it?", asked Alice.

"Why is a raven like a writing desk?", asked the Mad Hatter.

"I think I can answer that", said Alice.

"What is the answer?", said the March Hair.

"I do not know. I give up", said Alice.

"I do not know either", said the Mad Hatter.

The Mad Hatter started singing.

Then, the dormouse started singing in his sleep.

"Have some more tea", said the March Hair.

"I have not had any yet", said Alice, "so I cannot have more".

"You mean you cannot have less", said the Mad Hatter.

Alice did not know what to say, so she just helped herself to some tea.

"I want a clean cup", said the Mad Hatter. So, they all moved one place to the left.

"Is that the reason there are so many tea things here?", said Alice.

"Yes. It is always tea time here, so we just always move to the left."

The Mad Hatter was the only one who gained from the move, as he got a clean cup. Alice moved into the seat where the March Hair had been sitting.

The dormouse fell asleep again. The Mad Hatter and the March Hair started trying to put the dormouse into the teapot.

"Now if you ask me, I do not think . . .", said Alice.

"Then you should not talk", said the Mad Hatter.

Alice walked off. "I will never go there again", said Alice. "It is the stupidest tea party I have ever seen."

Alice saw a tree with a door in it. She decided to go in the door, and found herself in the same room where she had been when she first fell to the bottom of the rabbit hole.

This time she had the golden key and two pieces of mushroom that would make her bigger and smaller. She ate the mushrooms until she was one foot tall. She went through the little door and into the beautiful garden.

At the entrance to the garden, there was a rose tree that was growing white roses. There were three gardeners there, painting all the roses red.

The gardeners were all cards from a deck of cards. They were the seven, the five and the two of spades.

"Why are you painting the white roses red?", asked Alice.

The Two of Spades answered, "You see. We were supposed to plant a red rose tree here. We made a mistake and planted a white rose tree instead."

"If the Queen finds out, she will have our heads chopped off."

Just then, the Five cried out, "The Queen! The Queen!" They all three threw themselves down on the ground, face down. Alice looked around, because she wanted to see the Queen.

First came ten soldiers who were clubs, then ten soldiers who were diamonds, then ten children who were hearts. Next came the kings and the queens and among them the White Rabbit, who was smiling at everybody, but with a worried look on his face.

Last came the King and Queen of Hearts, along with the Knave of Hearts, who was carrying the crown of the King.

When they came to where Alice was standing, they stopped.

"Who is this?", said the Queen to the Knave of Hearts.

The Knave of Hearts only smiled and said nothing.

"Idiot!", said the Queen of Hearts.

Now, turning to Alice, "What is your name, child?", said the Queen.

"My name is Alice, so please your majesty", said Alice.

"And who are these?", said the Queen pointing to the three cards lying face down on the ground.

"How should I know?", said Alice.

"Off with her head", said the Queen of Hearts.

The King laid his hand on her arm and said, "Consider: She is only a child."

"Who are they", said the Queen, pointing to the three cards on the ground. "Turn them over."

The Knave of Hearts turned them over.

"Get up", cried the Queen. The three gardeners jumped up and began bowing to the Queen.

Turning to the rose tree, the Queen said, "What have you been doing?"

"May it please your majesty, we were trying . . . .", said the Two of Spades.

"I see! Off with their heads", said the Queen.

The group moved on except for three soldiers who stayed behind to execute the three gardeners.

Alice hid the three gardeners in a flower pot. The three soldiers searched but could not find them. Finally, they rejoined the group.

"Are their heads off?", asked the Queen.

"Their heads are gone", replied the soldiers.

"That's right!", shouted the Queen. "Can you play croquet?"

The three soldiers looked at Alice. "Yes", said Alice.

"Come on then", roared the Queen, and Alice joined the group.

Alice found herself walking next to the White Rabbit.

"Where is the Lady?", Alice asked.

"Hush", the White Rabbit said, whispering into the ear of Alice. "She is under a sentence of execution."

"Why?", asked Alice.

"She came rather late", answered the White Rabbit.

"Go to your places", shouted the Queen, and the game began.

It was a strange game. The croquet balls were small animals. The mallets were flamingos. The arches were soldiers doubled up on their hands and feet.

Alice had a lot of trouble playing this game. When she was just about to hit the ball with the flamingo, it would turn around and look at her. When it was ready again, the ball would get up and walk away. When both were ready, the soldiers who were arches would get up and walk somewhere else.

All of the players played at once without waiting for turns. The Queen kept running around shouting, "Off with your head! Off with your head!" Alice was wondering how anybody was left alive.

Alice saw something funny in the air. At first, she did not know what it was. Then she saw the teeth, then a grin, and then she saw that it was the Cheshire Cat.

Alice was happy that she had somebody to talk to. Finally the whole head appeared, but nothing else appeared.

"How are you doing?", said the Cheshire Cat.

"I do not think they play fair", said Alice. "They do not have any rules, and when my ball was going to hit the queen's ball, it just got up and ran away."

"Who are you talking to?", said the King, looking at the head of the Cheshire Cat.

"It is my friend, a Cheshire Cat", said Alice.

"Cats must not look at Kings", said the King. "It must be removed."

"Off with his head", said the Queen, without even looking around.

The King ran off to find a soldier.

Alice went back to the game. When she returned to the Cheshire Cat, a large crowd had gathered around it. There was a dispute between the soldier, the King and the Queen.

The soldier said that he cannot behead the head of the Cheshire Cat because it has no body.

The King said that anybody with a head has a body.

The Queen said if you do not do something soon, everybody will be beheaded. She had already ordered the execution of three players in the game.

They decided that Alice should settle this dispute, so they all told their case to Alice.

After hearing from everybody, Alice said, "The Cheshire Cat belongs to the Lady. You have to ask her."

"She is under a sentence to be killed", shouted the Queen. "Have her brought here."

By the time that the soldier had brought the Lady, the Cheshire Cat had disappeared again, so everybody went back to playing the game.

"You cannot think how glad I am to see you", said the Lady to Alice.

"It is love, it is love that makes the world go round", said the Lady.

"Somebody said that it was minding one's own business", said Alice, remembering that the Lady had said that on page 44.

The Queen came before them and said to the Lady, "Either you or your head will be off."

The Lady understood and left right away, leaving Alice with the Queen.

"Have you seen the Mock Turtle yet?", the Queen asked Alice. "Come on and I shall show you."

The Queen and Alice walked off. Alice could hear the King saying in a low voice to the soldiers behind them, "You are all pardoned."

The Queen took Alice to see the Griffin. "Get up and take this girl to see the Mock Turtle", said the Queen to the Griffin. "I must go to see some executions that I have ordered."

After the Queen had left, the Griffin said, "What Fun!"

"Why is it fun?", said Alice.

"It is all her fantasy. They never execute anybody", said the Griffin.

The Griffin took Alice to see the Mock Turtle, who was crying.

"Why is he so sad?", asked Alice.

"He is not sad. He cries when he is happy", answered the Griffin.

The Griffin and the Mock Turtle told Alice stories about themselves. They sang to Alice.

They sang about a dance they used to do with a lobster. When the dance was finished, they and the lobster would be thrown out to sea, and then they would all swim back.

Just as the Mock turtle was finishing his song, "The Trial is beginning", was heard in the distance.

"Come on", said the Griffin, taking Alice by the hand, and they ran to see the trial.

The King and Queen of Hearts were seated on their throne.

The White Rabbit was standing next to them, with a trumpet in hand.

The Knave of Hearts was standing before them in chains, being guarded by two soldiers.

There were 12 animals and birds in the jury box. One of them was Bill the Lizard.

Alice was happy to see that she knew everybody there.

The White Rabbit unfolded a big piece of paper and read out the charge:

"The Queen of Hearts, She Made Some Tarts
All on a Summer Day
The Knave of Hearts, he stole the tarts
And took them quite Away"

"Call the First Witness", said the King.

The White Rabbit blew on his trumpet and said, "First Witness".

The first witness was the Mad Hatter.

The Mad Hatter had a cup of tea and a biscuit in his hands.

"Excuse me for these, but I had not finished my tea when you called", said the Mad Hatter.

"When did you start it", asked the Queen.

"The Fourteenth of March", answered the Mad Hatter.

"No. It was the Fifteenth of March", said the March Hair.

"No. It was the Sixteenth", said the dormouse.

"Take off your hat", said the King to the Mad Hatter.

"I cannot", said the Mad Hatter. "It does not belong to me."

"Is it stolen?", asked the King.

"I make hats to sell. None belong to me. I am a hatter", said the Mad Hatter.

"Give me your evidence, or I will have you executed", said the King.

At this time, Alice noticed that she was growing.

"I am a poor man", said the Mad Hatter, "and I had not finished my tea."

"What did the dormouse say", asked a member of the jury.

"I cannot remember", said the Mad Hatter.

"You must remember, or I will have you killed", said the King.

"I am a poor man", the Mad Hatter said again. The Mad Hatter was so nervous that his shoes fell off.

"Then you may sit down", said the king.

"I would rather finish my tea", said the Mad Hatter.

"Call the next witness", said the King.

"You may take his head off outside", said the Queen, but the Mad Hatter had already run away so fast that he had even left his shoes behind.

The White Rabbit fumbled with his list. Alice was very surprised when the White Rabbit called out, "Alice!".

Alice forgot that she had been growing. Alice had grown so big, that when she stood up, she upset the jury box. All the jurors fell to the ground. Alice tried to pick them up and put them back. She had at first put in Bill the Lizard upside down, so she set him upright.

"What do you know about this business?", said the King.

"Nothing", said Alice.

"Nothing whatever?", said the King.

"Nothing whatever", said Alice

"That is very important", said the King to the jurors.

"Unimportant", said the White Rabbit.

"Unimportant, I meant", said the King.

All this time, Alice had been growing.

"Silence", said the King. "All persons more than a mile high must leave the court."

"I am not a mile high", said Alice.

"You are two miles high", said the Queen.

The King turned to the Jury. "Consider your verdict", he said.

"Wait, there is more evidence", said the White Rabbit, holding up a piece of paper.

"What does it say?", said the King.

"It is not signed", said the White Rabbit.

"Since it is not signed, you can not prove that I wrote it", said the Knave of Hearts.

"That proves that you are guilty", said the King. "An honest man would have signed it."

"It says the tarts are right here", said the White Rabbit, reading the paper.

"Yes. The Tarts are here, they have been here all along", said the King, pointing to the tarts on the table in front of him.

"Never", said the Queen, throwing a bottle of ink at Bill the Lizard.

"We must have a verdict", said the King.

"No. Sentence first, then the verdict", said the Queen.

"Stuff and nonsense", said Alice. "The verdict must come before the sentence."

"Off with her head", shouted the Queen of Hearts.

"Who cares about you? You are nothing but a pack of cards", said Alice.

The whole pack of cards came flying up into the air and came down on Alice. Alice gave off a scream, weaving her arms as the cards came flying towards her. Suddenly Alice woke up, and found herself lying on the river bank, with her head in her sister's lap.

"Wake up, Alice", said her sister.

Alice woke up.

"I had a most curious dream", said Alice.

Alice told everything she had dreamed to her sister. Her sister wrote it all down and put it in a book.

And this is the book.

THE END

If you did not understand this story, do not feel badly, because nobody else can understand it either.

Later, Alice had another adventure. I will not tell you the whole story now, but here is the most important part.

Alice was playing a game of chess and looking at herself in a looking glass.

On the other side of the glass, everything was backwards.

Alice went through the looking glass.

When she came out of the other side of the looking glass, everything went in the opposite direction.

Alice found herself in a forest where the flowers could talk to her and were singing beautiful songs.

Alice met a Red Queen. There was a chess game being played. The pieces in the game were people, animals and birds.

Alice asked the Red Queen to make her a pawn in the game.

Alice became a pawn in the game.

Alice took a train that moved her two squares forward, like a pawn does on the first move in chess.

After Alice moved two squares forward, she met a nice Fawn there.

However, the Fawn ran away after she realized that Alice was a human child.

Alice moved one square forward, where she met Tweedle-Dum and Tweedle-Dee.

They told her the story of The Walrus and The Carpenter.

"The time has come the Walrus said
To think of many things.
Of shoes and ships and sealing wax
Of cabbages and kings
And why the seas are boiling hot
And whether pigs have wings"

Alice knew that the seas are not boiling hot and that pigs do not have wings, so she moved on to the next square.

There, she met Humpty Dumpty sitting on a wall.

Alice already knew the story of Humpty Dumpty.

She knew that he would fall off the wall, but Humpty Dumpty said that he was sure that All the Kings Horses and All the Kings Men would put Humpty Dumpty together again.

Soon, Humpty Dumpty fell off the wall. The King called all his horses and all his men, but they could not put Humpty Dumpty together again.

Alice moved forward to another square, and there she met the White Knight.

The White Knight said that he would help Alice reach the eighth square and become a queen.

The White Knight kept looking backwards and kept falling off his horse.

Finally, Alice reached the eighth square and became a Queen.

Now that Alice was a Queen, she needed to be in a Palace.

Alice went to the palace but the door was closed.

Alice knocked on the door. A servant looked out and said, "No answers until next week", and shut the door.

Alice knocked and knocked. Nobody answered the door again.

Finally, an old frog came over and kicked open the door. The frog said, "It is your palace now. Just go in."

Alice went in the door and found people singing to her, welcoming her as the new Queen.

Then Alice woke up from her dream again.

THE VERY END

Alice in Wonderland Made Simple for Kids

By Sam Sloan, adopted from the Original by Lewis Carroll

"Alice in Wonderland" was first published in 1865 and "Alice Through the Looking Glass" was first published in 1871. There is no copyright any longer, so everybody can write their own stories about Alice and draw their own pictures of what they think Alice and her friends looked like.

My six-year-old daughter likes to talk to her imaginary friend, Alice, on her toy telephone. I decided to write this book so that it would be possible for my daughter to read it.

There are many books about Alice. There is also a song. It is called "*White Rabbit*". It is a famous song of the 1960s. You can find it on youtube.com and play it over and over again to hear about Alice.

The original Alice story was written by a mathematician. It is filled with puzzles, riddles and logical problems. It is too difficult for children to understand and most adults cannot understand it either, so I have tried to re-write it to make it easier for children to read and understand. I have kept all of the main characters. I have used all of the original drawings by John Tenniel. I have not changed the story, except that I have made it shorter.

Many readers will not be satisfied with my simplified version of *Alice in Wonderland*. Never fear, because there are more than one hundred books about Alice. You can read them until you find one you like. Perhaps the best is "*The Annotated Alice*" by Martin Gardner.

You can also go to movies about Alice. Walt Disney made a movie, but many people do not like it because he mixed up the two stories and he made changes in the story. Do not blame Walt for that, because it is difficult to make this book into a movie. At least he tried. One of the changes Walt Disney made was at the end where he put Alice on Trial. In the original book, it was the Jack of Hearts on trial for stealing the tarts from Queen of Hearts. Also, Walt Disney left out the Duchess completely. Here, I call her the Lady instead of the Duchess, because the word "Duchess" is rarely used any more, and especially not in America.

Queen Victoria, who was Queen of England at the time this story was published, liked the story. It is good that she did, because the drawings of the Queen of Hearts looked like her and the King of Hearts was like her husband, Prince Albert. If she had not liked the story, she would have chopped off the head of the author.

The best part is you can write your own Alice stories and make your own books about Alice, because there is no copyright any longer. That is why everybody is making books and movies about Alice now.

ISBN 0-923891-91-9

Ishi Press International
1664 Davidson Avenue, Suite 1B
Bronx NY 10453-7877
USA
917-507-7226
Printed in the United States of America

6052543R0

Made in the USA
Lexington, KY
12 July 2010